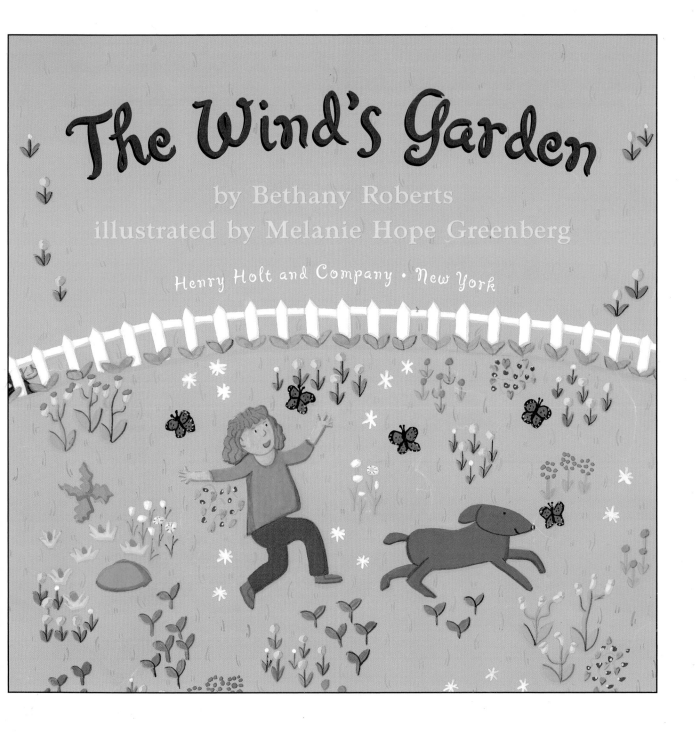

The Wind's Garden

by Bethany Roberts

illustrated by Melanie Hope Greenberg

Henry Holt and Company • New York

Henry Holt and Company, LLC
Publishers since 1866
115 West 18th Street
New York, New York 10011

Henry Holt is a registered trademark
of Henry Holt and Company, LLC

Published in Canada by Fitzhenry & Whiteside Ltd.,
195 Allstate Parkway, Markham, Ontario L3R 4T8.

Library of Congress Cataloging-in-Publication Data
Roberts, Bethany.
The wind's garden / by Bethany Roberts; illustrated by Melanie Hope Greenberg.
Summary: A child and the wind plant very different gardens.
[1. Gardens—Fiction. 2. Wind—Fiction.] I. Greenberg, Melanie Hope, ill. II. Title.
PZ7.R5396 Wi 2001 [E]—dc21 99-47348

ISBN 0-8050-6367-6
First Edition—2001
The artist used gouache on 140-pound watercolor paper
to create the illustrations for this book.
Printed in the United States of America on acid-free paper. ∞

10 9 8 7 6 5 4 3 2 1

To the green thumbs in my family:
happy gardening!
—B. R.

To the divine Shakti,
the Mother of All That Is;
special thanks to Andrea Demetropoulos
—M. H. G.

This spring,
I planted a garden.

The wind planted a garden, too.

I dug the dirt,
and raked things smooth.

Then I planted my seeds.

The wind just blew.
It swirled around,
throwing seeds to the ground,
here and there
and everywhere.

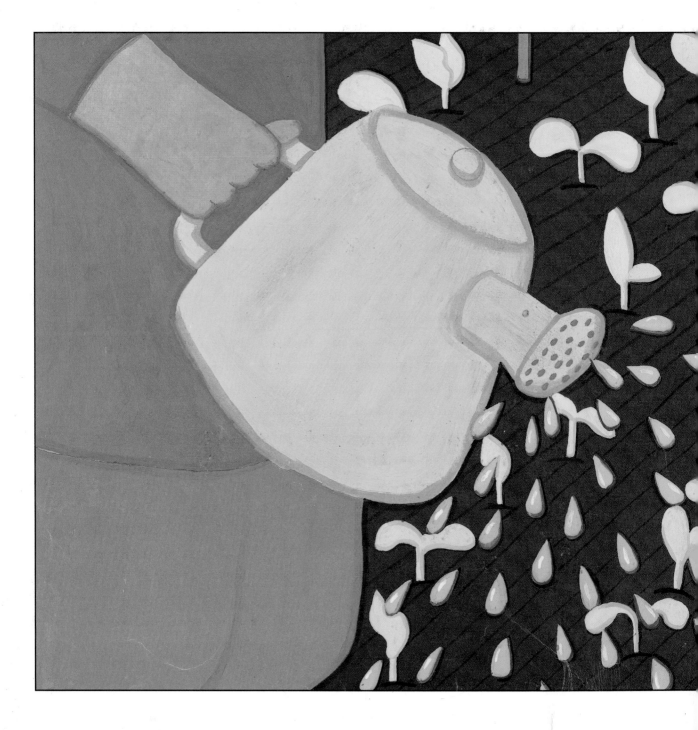

I watered my seeds.
The wind didn't water.

But the rain splashed down
on the dry, parched ground
of the wind's garden,
and my garden, too.

I pulled the weeds.

The wind didn't weed.
Its garden just grew.

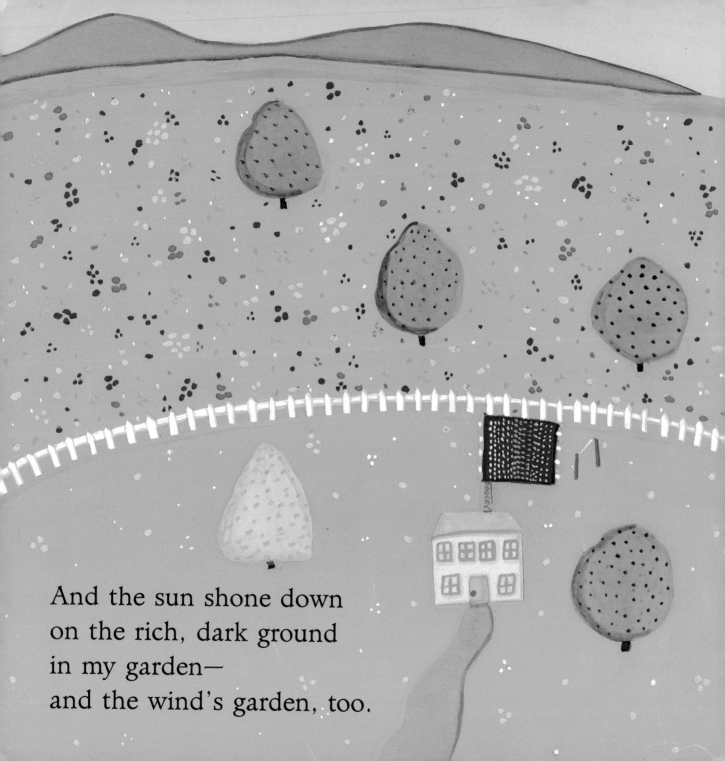

And the sun shone down
on the rich, dark ground
in my garden—
and the wind's garden, too.

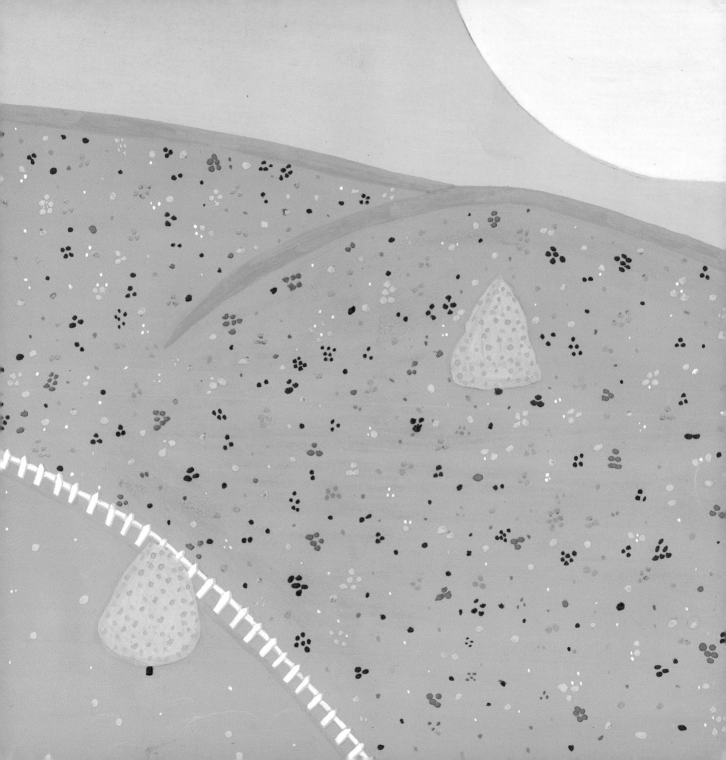

Bees buzzed
and butterflies flew.
Our gardens GREW

and GREW

and GREW!

My garden . . .

and the wind's garden, too.

Author's Note

Your Garden

You can grow a garden, too.

Some easy seeds to start with are zinnias, bachelor buttons, and **marigolds**.

In the spring, plant your seeds in a sunny place with good soil. **Water the** seeds, pull the weeds, and watch your garden grow.

The Wind's Garden

You can help the wind.

When a dandelion flower turns from a sunny yellow to a white puffy **little** cloud, pick it up and blow. The seeds will sail away, like tiny parachutes. If the seeds land in a spot with good soil, they will grow.

Many wildflowers and other plants scatter their seeds with the help of the wind. Look for them in cracks in sidewalks, in vacant lots, along roadsides, in meadows and fields, and even in your own backyard.